CRAVINGS

D E McCluskey

D E McCluskey

CRAVINGS

Copyright © 2021 by D E McCluskey

The moral right of the author has been asserted
All characters and events in this publication,
other than those clearly in the public domain,
are fictitious and any resemblance to real persons,
living or dead, is purely coincidental

All rights are reserved

No part of this publication may be reproduced,
stored in a retrieval system, or transmitted in any form
by any means, without the prior permission, in writing of
the publisher, nor be otherwise circulated in any form of binding or cover other than
that of which it was
published and without a similar condition including this
condition being imposed on the subsequent purchaser.
ISBN 978-1-914381-08-9

Dammaged Production
www.dammaged.com

Cravings

To all the pregnant women out there…

I can't even begin to feel your pain.

D E McCluskey

Cravings

1.

'SO, THERE IT is. There's the head, the spinal column, the little legs.' The nurse pointed to a tiny flashing light on the screen. 'And do you see that pulse there? Well, that's the essence of the little life inside you. That's the heart beating. I'm pleased to tell you that you have a healthy little…'

She paused.

The lady on the bed, with her stomach exposed, was beaming at the screen, as was the man next to her grasping her hand.

'Do you want me to continue?' she asked, a knowing look on her face.

The couple looked at each other, laughed, and shook their heads. 'No!' the mother whispered. Her voice spoke her confirmation, but her eyes told a different story, one that the nurse had seen time and time again.

'We figured that you don't get many nice surprises in life, and whichever way this goes, it'll be a nice surprise,' the husband said, tearing his gaze from the computer screen, and squeezed his wife's hand.

'I understand,' the nurse replied, nodding and removing the scanning device, turning the screen blank. 'And I agree,' she whispered. 'All you need to know is that you have a healthy little life inside you. Now, if you want physical copies of the scan, then we ask for a small donation to the hospital of five pounds.'

'Oh, yeah. Of course, we want a couple of them,' the husband said reaching for his wallet.

The nurse smiled, accepting the money. 'You two get cleaned up, and I'll see you in the reception.'

Five minutes later, Roger and Sarah Todd were standing in the reception of the maternity clinic, cuddling into each other's embrace. Even though they were both into their thirties, they looked like two loved up teenagers.

Teenagers who had just received the best news ever.

'There you go,' the nurse said with a smile, handing over two strips of black and white images and ten pounds in change.

Roger held up his hand. 'No, please keep the twenty, call it a donation. You've given us the best news today! It's only fair that we give something back.'

Cravings

'Thank you, Mr Todd, that's very generous.' The nurse's attention then moved to Sarah, who was gawping at the scans. 'So, mummy, have you had any cravings yet?'

Sarah looked up. 'Huh?'

'Cravings? You know, any unusual patterns on what you want to eat? The baby has certain needs and requirements, and whatever it wants, you have to provide.'

'Oh, I read up about them, of course, but most people seem to think they're a myth. Made up stories to amuse people at dinner parties.'

The nurse raised her eyebrows. 'Oh no, believe me, they're real. When I was pregnant, all I wanted to eat was sardines.' She pulled a face and shook her head. 'The thought of eating sardines right now!'

Both parents laughed. 'Well, we're doing this by the book. No tinned fish for this one. It's fresh fruit and fibre all the way,' Roger replied.

The nurse nodded. She'd seen over eagerness before. All the best intentions were usually discarded by the time the first cravings kicked in. 'Well, sometimes it's not up to you, but I wish you both the best of luck, and I'll see you again in…' she looked at the appointment register before her, 'ten weeks. Congratulations and good luck!'

'Thank you. For everything.'

As the nurse watched the happy couple make their way out of the unit, she shook her head, the wry smile back on her face. 'Good luck with the fruit and fibre,' she mumbled before looking at the rota to see who was covering for lunch.

All the talk of sardines had made her hungry. Absently, she put her hand on her stomach and felt around, shaking her head. She was not one-hundred-percent sure that she didn't want sardines on toast.

The thought worried her.

2.

'I DON'T GIVE that cravings thing any credence!' Roger said as they drove home. 'The book says that all the body needs is a healthy regime with as many natural vitamins and minerals as it can get. Don't you think?' He turned towards Sarah in the passenger seat.

Even though her bump wasn't really showing yet, she was lying back with her hands on her stomach. Her eyes were closed.

'Are you OK, honey?'

Her smile was dreamy. 'Yeah, I'm just so happy, that's all.'

He smiled and took her hand.

'I'm hungry though.'

'Well, that's normal. We're nearly home. I'll rustle you up a delicious smoothie when we get in. I bought some fresh spinach this morning.'

'Fuck your spinach, Rog, I want a burger.'

His brow ruffled as he regarded her; there was almost a look of horror on his face. 'A burger? Since when do we eat burgers?'

She shrugged her shoulders. 'I'm sorry but I just fancy one. Stop at the nearest drive-through, will you?'

'Sarah, I'm not stopping for a burger. You've got a responsibility to our baby inside you. I'm not about to let you feed it up with a load of shit.'

As he uttered this last word, a rumble came from her stomach, and her hands gravitated towards her belly. She looked at him and laughed.

'Oh, for fucks sake, I've got a good mind to report that nurse for putting the idea of cravings in your head,' he tutted as he turned the car towards the nearest drive-through.

Cravings

3.

THE BURGER HAD been delicious, but it didn't satisfy the empty feeling inside her. She needed something else, she just didn't know what.

Roger was in the kitchen, spinning something green into a plastic jug.

'What are you making?' she asked with disinterest.

'Your dinner! After your little, shall we call it a diversion, this afternoon, I thought it best to get something healthy inside you.'

Sarah looked at the goo inside the jug and her stomach churned, disturbing the greasy meat inside it. 'I don't think I could stomach any of that Rog. That burger is lying heavy.'

'I'm not surprised!' he laughed. 'I just hope you learned a lesson from it.'

Anger flashed over her face for a moment as as a cramp hit her, overtaking the emotion. Her hands grasped at her bump, and a grimace spread across her face.

'Are you OK?' Roger asked, racing towards her.

She brushed away his overly cautious advance as she headed towards the door. 'Every time I get a pain, it doesn't mean I'm losing the baby you know,' she snapped.

'I know, but after everything…'

'I think you were right about that burger, though. I just need to…' Without finishing her sentence, she darted out of the kitchen, heading for the stairs.

She only just made it as the pains in her stomach intensified. She fumbled at the buttons on her jeans and fought an embittered campaign with the zipper. Finally free of her constraints, she pulled her trousers down seconds before the pains were too unbearable to hold.

An explosion happened beneath her.

The feeling of relief was instantaneous as hot liquid squirted from her, leaving a not unpleasant sting, but also a blessed empty feeling. The smell was hideous. It reminded her of the burger she had eaten earlier, but with a musty, herby essence to it. With ample toilet roll, she slipped her hand beneath and attempted to wipe, when another pain wracked through her.

Cravings

There was another hot squirt. This one gushed over the hand that she was wiping with. The wet warmth on her fingers felt strange, greasy. She quickly removed the hand, attempting to get it out of the way in case of another squirt, but in her hurry, she caught her hand on the side of the bowl. Her fingernail bent right back, and she felt it snap where it met the skin of her finger. The pain from the snag was more intense than the cramps had been.

Without thinking, she did something that she'd done her entire life, entirely without thinking. She put the finger in her mouth.

The same finger that was, at present, dripping with warm, semi-liquified excrement fresh from her bowels.

The moment the finger was inside, it stopped throbbing and began to feel better.

She sighed, closed her eyes, and relaxed.

Realisation dawned on her, and she jerked the offending hand from her mouth, sending wet shit from her fingers splashing over the white tiles of the bathroom floor.

~~~~

The brown spatter was an accusation. The dark stain was stark against the white of the floor.

The same slimy solution was also in her mouth! Before she could think about spitting it out, she gagged. The thick liquid slid down her throat, and she had no option but to swallow.

The feeling of the waste sliding down her throat was abhorrent, and she gagged again.

Suddenly, her stomach eased.

It was an odd moment that she likened to a storm passing over the sea. One minute there was turmoil, the next, calm.

She was left with a nasty feeling in her mouth; but, as she thought about it, she was no longer sure if it *was* disgusting, or if she'd just been programmed to think that way. Guiltily, she clicked her tongue against the roof of her mouth and swallowed the remaining residue.

It wasn't bad at all. In fact, it was rather sweet.

She looked at her hand, still covered in brown, pungent slime, and her stomach grumbled.

The beige, semi-transparent sludge was clinging to her fingers. Her stomach growled again, like a wild animal sensing that the food it needed, that it craved, was close.

She shook her head, not understanding why she was even thinking about what she was about to do. She moved her hand closer to her face and sniffed. The cloying stink travelled through her nostrils and down into her stomach. Expecting to feel revolted, she was surprised at how enticing it smelt, almost like a broth.

The nearer it got, the more her stomach growled, aching for it.

Slowly, and not without disgust, she put the slimed fingers into her mouth and sucked the pungent juice from them. Before she knew it, she was lapping at the other fingers, sucking at the spaces between them, and licking her brown smeared palms.

It was amazing; her stomach agreed with her. She was moaning as she slurped her own ablution from her fingers.

'Sarah, are you OK in there?'

Roger's voice snapped her out of her filthy reverie. 'Sarah?'

'I'm OK, Rog,' she replied, wiping the filth from her chin. 'I'm just finishing up. You were right about that burger, no more of them for me.'

'There's no… erm, blood, is there?'

Sarah looked at her now clean fingers and shook her head. 'No, Rog, there's no blood,' she confirmed. *But a whole fucking load of crazy,* she finished in her head.

'Thank God for that! You had me worried there. Right, I'll be downstairs finishing off this smoothie. All the ingredients mashed together makes it look like shit.'

Sarah wiped herself clean and flushed the toilet. She then looked in the mirror. there was a brown smear from the corner of her mouth, down over her chin. Appalled, she ran the taps and scrubbed her face, pulling her tongue out to clean that too. She then took her toothbrush, squeezed out a blob of paste, and proceeded to scrub her mouth. She rinsed and then gargled with mouthwash for a good two minutes before spitting it out. She looked at her face and noticed that her skin was glowing. Her cheeks were flushed with colour and she looked… healthy.

Cravings

4.

A FEW WEEKS passed without any reoccurrence of the madness of that night. Her bump was now pronounced, and she felt better, healthier, than she had in a long while.

The toilet incident had passed into memory, rationalised as merely a moment of insanity. Anxiety; vile, but anxiety, nonetheless. After the years of wanting, trying, and ultimately failing, the fear of this baby not being healthy had caused her sanity to lapse. Now she was eating well, exercising, and protecting the beautiful life that was growing inside her.

Work took up most of her worry now. The company was merging with a larger, French company, and rumours abounded. Redeployment, redundancies, restructuring. The three Rs, they'd been branded. She was agonising as she'd been in the company long enough to qualify for the nine-month, full pay, maternity leave, but she knew if the merger passed before she went on that leave, there was a chance she could either lose her job or she would have to re-apply, and the conditions of work she currently enjoyed would change significantly.

It was a period of stress for her, and she wasn't reacting to it very well.

She'd rushed breakfast and was really regretting it now. The cramps in her stomach were coming like angry waves crashing against the rocky shoreline of her belly, making her feel awful, and alarmed. Ever since they'd found out that the baby was healthy and, well, alive, she and Roger had panicked at every little twinge and ache. So, as she listened to her stomach draining, and the ache in her bowel growing, she relaxed, secure in the knowledge that it was just a motion and not a miscarriage.

Her stomach drained again. The growl was louder this time and was accompanied with an uncomfortable feeling below. Looking around the room, she hoped that no-one had heard, but was embarrassed to see everyone in the corresponding booths standing, looking in at her. Luckily, they were all women, and they were laughing.

'I think you best get going!' one of them chuckled.

'And quick! It sounds like you're going to have an accident. Mummies-to-be don't have the choice to hold it in, darling,' another giggled.

Without a word, she hurried off towards the toilets.

Cravings

Thankfully, they were empty. The stalls along the wall were vacant; their doors hanging open like the mouths of hungry monsters waiting to get their fill of waste.

She chose the one furthest from the entrance and slammed the door behind her. She had to slide the lock into its holder twice as, in her rush, she missed it the first time. Then she fumbled down the elasticated waist of her leggings. With maybe half a second to spare, her bottom touched the seat. Her stomach cried out one last time, then a wave of wet, warm faeces squirted out.

The instant relief was phenomenal.

She rolled toilet paper around her hand and proceeded to wipe. Unfortunately, she misjudged the amount she needed, and her finger broke through the sodden paper. As she was in mid-wipe, there was nothing that she could do to stop the momentum, and the length of her finger passed across her moist button.

With a grimace, she removed her hand and looked at it. It was almost completely beige, with small white bits of paper hanging from it.

She was about to wipe it off when her stomach called to her. The noise was different this time. There was a longing to it, as if it was pining for the shit that was covering her finger. Inside, she cringed, baulking at the thought of what her sudden craving was about to make her do. Outwardly, she licked her lips. *What the fuck?* she thought. *Don't make me do this!* She was fighting a losing battle, completely under the control of whatever was inside her.

In a true dichotomy, she pondered her fingers. The stink coming from them, and from the bowl beneath her, was disgusting, disturbing, and alluring in equal measures. Her insides were roiling, but she could no more help herself than she could have helped expelling the filth in the first place.

Slowly, she brought her hand closer to her face. The sickly sweetness of the residue was feeding her hunger. *No, not hunger… starvation!*

She closed her eyes.

Her whole body shook as she stuck her tongue out of her mouth and licked the wet finger.

It was cold, and there was a strange gritty texture to it, like seeds. It was so much different from the juice she'd tasted last time.

Once her finger was clean, and she had scraped everything out from beneath her fingernails, she wiped herself again, fighting the impulse to chew on and swallow the used paper. Ultimately, she won that struggle! She flushed the toilet and almost fell out of the cubicle.

She got to the sink, ran the cold water, and began to rinse her mouth, looking into the mirror as she did. Her teeth were stained, and there were black bits, like seeds, stuck between them. She rubbed at them; she needed them to be clean, needed all evidence of her madness eradicated.

The door opened and someone entered the toilets. It was Jolene from accounts.

'Oh, hey, Sarah.' She smiled before her face changed. 'Oh, my God! Are you OK? Don't take this the wrong way, but you look like shit.'

Sarah smiled at the irony of the words. She held her hand up and breathed in deep. 'No, I'm fine,' she laughed. 'It's just a touch of morning sickness, that's all.'

Jolene smiled. 'Have you been having cravings?'

Sarah looked at her, and her face fell. 'What?'

Jolene's own face changed then as Sarah's breath hit her. Her eyes widened as she coughed back a gag. 'Oh, nothing! I just wondered if you were having cravings and coming in here for a little bit of *illicit* time, that's all.'

'What are you talking about?'

She pointed to a small brown stain on Sarah's shirt, next to her buttons. 'I thought you'd been eating chocolate in the toilets, that's all.'

Sarah looked down at the stain. It was a small beige swab of shit on her otherwise pristine white blouse. The stain mocked her.

'Oh!' she laughed. 'You know what it's like? When the baby wants something…'

'Yeah, I got pilchards! Fucking pilchards! My breath stank for the whole of the pregnancy. Chris wouldn't come anywhere near me for the whole term. I was a horny little bitch too…' she laughed and lightly slapped Sarah's arm. She grimaced as another whiff of Sarah's stink wafted over her. 'Anyway, nature calls, eh?' she said, backing away into the stall that Sarah had recently vacated.

Sarah watched as the door locked before looking at herself in the mirror. The stain was obvious; glaringly so. She dabbed a little water on it, knowing only too well that it would only serve to make the stain bigger.

Then she caught a whiff of her breath. *Jesus, no wonder Jolene got away so fast!*

Her mouth was foul. She rummaged through her handbag, hoping there might be some mints or maybe gum inside.

Luckily, there was one piece of gum languishing at the bottom of the bag. It looked like it had been there for months. The grey tablet was covered in fluff. She looked at it, hesitating before putting it in her mouth, not really wanting something as filthy as that anywhere near her. *Oh, my God! After what I've just done, I'm worried about putting a fucking mouldy piece of gum in my mouth?*

Cravings

She popped it in and began to chew. It was soft, but there was still plenty of flavour in it.

Stepping out of the toilets, she breathed in deeply and realised that she needed more gum. The smell of the shit must have been either in her nostrils, or even all over her, because it followed her out.

'Girls, would you mind if I just popped to the shops? I've got bad indigestion and need something to calm my stomach.'

No one minded at all, and she was glad of the escape.

She reached the elevators, pressed the button, and waited. Eventually, the doors opened, and an embarrassed young man looked at her before stepping out and hurrying off towards the offices with his head hung low. The moment the elevator doors closed; she understood. The poor man had off loaded a rather unpleasant bout of gas in the confines of the carriage. She gagged as the stink enveloped her. But, as it lingered, she realised that she was reacting to a programmed response to the smell, one that had been ingrained in her since childhood. Now that she'd changed, the smell was actually... delightful.

It smelt like roast chicken.

That thought made her stomach growl again.

She looked at her watch, it was very nearly lunch time, and she longed for something substantial in her belly. The man's lingering smell was making her mouth water.

She reluctantly exited the elevator into the foyer and made her way towards the shop. She bought two packs of gum and a large chicken sandwich and took an empty table in the seating area. As she unwrapped her lunch, her stomach screamed for the food. She attempted to satiate it by eating it as quickly as she could.

As soon as it was in her mouth, her stomach disapproved. The bread felt heavy, and the chicken was too dry.

Frustrated, she dropped the uneaten remains back into the wrapper and looked all around the foyer. Her stomach was raging now! Her eyes drifted towards the public toilets by the lifts, and something inside her compelled her towards them.

What the fuck am I doing? she thought as she stepped inside the cool, darkened room. She entered a vacant cubicle, removed her leggings, and sat down.

She attempted to go, but nothing happened, her stomach was too stubborn to release anything.

Then she heard the flushing of another cubicle.

Her heart began to beat double time, as the aroma of someone else's ablutions drifted over her.

Cravings

She waited, listening as the door opened and the occupant left. Holding her breath, she heard whoever it was wash her hands, and then... nothing!

Come on, come on. What the hell are you doing, bitch? she scolded under her breath. Eventually the hand-dryer kicked in, and she released her sigh, slowly but surely. The hunger pangs were crippling her as the fragrance, travelling on the warm air eddies from the hand dryer, continued to waft over her. Then they left! Relief washed through her. She unlocked the door and was about exit when someone else entered. With a silent curse, she closed the door again and locked it.

'Holy fuck!' the newcomer cried as she entered the stall vacated by the previous occupant. 'Some people are just...'

The cubicle door slammed and the woman stormed out of the bathroom. Sarah's stomach yelled at her, ordering her to get a move on before anyone else could come in in ruin the moment. She unbolted the door and darted into the next cubicle.

What she found there turned her stomach *and* heightened her excitement in equal measures.

The bowl was a disgrace. There were brown slicks down either side, and the water had a coffee, swampy look to it. The single flush the woman had made had not been anywhere near powerful enough to compensate her discharge.

Silently, Sarah thanked her.

Lurking in the murk of the bowl was something she could just about make out, and her mouth watered. It was disgusting and beautiful; she was repulsed and attracted.

She knew what side was going to win.

Without further ado, she knelt on the wet floor and gripped the grimy porcelain bowl with both hands. Moving her head forwards, peering into the murky filth below her, she took a deep sniff. The smell was intoxicating. It stung her nostrils, causing tears to well. Her stomach howled again for the indecent goodness within her reach. She ran a finger down the sides, scooping the residue that was clinging there. Revulsion tore through her, mixed with desire, and her mouth filled with saliva in anticipation of the foul chocolate matter hitting her stomach.

She raised the finger, eyeing someone else's shit as if it was an hors-d'oeuvre in a fancy restaurant. She licked her lips and cringed. She wanted, no, she *needed* this disgusting glob of who-knew-whose waste in her stomach, and she needed it now.

Closing her eyes, she sucked her finger.

It was a taste explosion. There was a nutty taste to it, and something else; something like a secret ingredient, something she couldn't put her finger on. She guessed it must have been because it came from someone else's colon. *I wonder if everyone has their*

Cravings

own taste? she thought as she cleaned her digit. She dipped her hand again and again, until the residue on the side of the bowl was almost gone.

With the first course over, her stomach, and the growing baby inside it, told her they were ready for more.

With no hesitation, she delved her hand into the muddy waters and fished around for the prize that she knew was skulking somewhere within. Eventually, she found it. It was soft and cold in her hands. She knew she would have to play gently with this thing if any of its grimy goodness was going to be enjoyed.

She cupped the length of the stool, supporting it, before lifting it out of the water as if it was a delicate newborn baby. As it surfaced, she watched with dismay as a chunk broke off and splash back into the depths. *I'll get that in a moment,* she thought, as she brought her prize closer to her mouth.

She couldn't resist breathing in its aroma, its bouquet. It stunk! The stench was what she'd imagine an abattoir to smell like many months after being abandoned. But it was what her baby needed, and it was what her baby was going to get; besides, she wanted it herself now.

Lifting the dripping turd to her mouth, she opened her wet lips. Another chunk broke, splashing back into the water, and soaking her now less-than-white blouse. She no longer cared. She had one job to do, and that job was to provide her child with everything it needed to grow.

She ate the stranger's shit.

There were lumps in it! She had to press them down between her tongue and her teeth, in order to swallow them. Something crunched, and she was amazed to feel the sting of an almost complete peppercorn fill her mouth. The strong taste overpowered the wet shit on her tongue, but only for a moment.

Swallow after swallow of the gross goodness slid down her throat, and she groaned in satisfaction and pleasure.

Looking like a child after an epic Easter-egg hunt, she sat back and wiped her mouth, spreading a moist skid mark up her sleeve and over her cheeks. She grinned in satisfaction. The pains in her stomach receded, and she was finally able to relax.

The door to the toilets opened again, and her head whipped around, acutely aware that she was sitting on the wet floor of the cubicle. As she got herself back up onto the seat, she heard someone mumble something along the lines of 'Jesus Christ!' before swiftly leaving.

She was caked in filth. Her blouse was soaked, and there was a large swipe of brown up one of her sleeves. Her hands were coated in slime, and she had inadvertently wiped it over her leggings.

Cravings

She quickly licked her hands clean before wiping the rest of her face. There were clumps of faeces in her hair. Reaching her mostly clean hand into her bag, she pulled out a bobble and tied her hair back. Then, unlocking the cubicle door, she looked around. There was a door in the corner, and she wrenched it open. Inside were mops and brushes, exactly what she needed.

She took a brush and wedged it against the handle on the door, effectively locking herself inside, before stripping off her wet clothing. Resisting the urge to suck the sweet filth, she rinsed them under the tap. She looked in the mirror and winced. Her face looked like she'd been applying false tan while drunk. There were thick, brown swathes across her cheeks and lips. She licked at the drying scum, cleaning some of it off but leaving her face needing a through wash.

Once her shirt was clean-ish, she held it under the dryer for a few moments, then peeled off her soiled leggings. She did the same with them before washing her face and hands and stuffing a wad of gum into her mouth. Feeling half-normal, she left the toilets.

There were some odd looks from people as she exited, mostly due to her wet, disheveled appearance.

Taking her mobile phone, she rang the office. 'I think I'm going to have to go home. I'm not feeling too good,' she lied. After reassuring them that it was nothing to worry about, she exited the building and headed for the car park.

Her head was dizzy. How could she do something so disgusting, debasing, unsanitary, and not to mention insane?

The stink in her hair followed her to the car. She wanted to feel revolted but couldn't. It was as if something inside was telling her she needed it.

When she got home, she ran a bath, put her clothes in the washing machine, and scrubbed out her mouth, almost to the point of bleeding. When her hair was clean, she washed it again, just to make sure that everything was out of it.

Finally clean, she flopped into bed and put the pillow tight over her face and screamed. She could still smell the toilet in her hair as she drifted into a troubled sleep.

5.

SARAH WAS NOW another few weeks further along, and there had been no more vile cravings. She ate healthily, she exercised when she could, and she even managed to secure her job, and the maternity leave, after the merger.

Everything was going great. There were no unexpected surprises, and the doctors in the neonatal said her baby was healthy and developing well within the expected boundaries.

It seemed that she was stress free.

Until Roger decided to go out one Friday evening.

She was into her seventh month and had left work the week before. Roger had phoned and told her that he was going out on an evening meeting with new clients who were over from America. 'It might get a little rowdy, and I might be late,' he informed her. 'They're from Texas, and they don't do things by halves over there.'

She assured him it was OK, even going so far as telling him that she could use a little space anyway, she was going to have a soak in the bath and get an early night. 'But please, sleep in the spare room if you're coming in drunk; don't wake me up.'

He agreed and off he went.

Sarah spent the night pampering herself—a long soak, shaving her legs (where she could reach), and applying a beauty mask—before taking herself up to bed, after a brief, drunken conversation with her husband.

Almost instantly, she fell into a deep sleep, only to be awakened, rudely, a few hours later by her buzzing mobile phone. It was flashing an unknown number. In a state of panic, she looked at the clock. It read one-thirteen a.m. Her heart raced as she glared at the glowing screen. It rang off, but instantly rang again. Something inside her told her that she needed to answer, and she was glad she did.

'My apologies for ringing this late into the night, but can I ask if I'm speaking to Mrs. Todd?' the officious male voice on the other end of the line asked.

'Erm, yes. I'm Sarah Todd. Can I ask who's calling, please?' Panic was set in her voice.

'Of course, I'm sorry. My name's Doctor Powell. I'm calling from the Royal hospital. I'm afraid your husband has taken a rather nasty fall. He's inebriated and has been admitted. He was calling for you, and as he informed us that you're seven months pregnant, he wanted us to let you know that he's OK. We'll keep him in overnight. Will you or someone else be able to get him in the morning?'

'Yes! Yes, of course. Do you need anything from me right now?'

'No, you relax. He's in our care now, and he's asleep. I can't see him waking any time within the next few hours. He'll be good 'til the morning.'

6.

SARAH LOOKED AT the clock. It now read five forty-six. 'Might as well get up,' she mumbled, throwing the sheets off her. 'Not going back to sleep now.'

That was when she noticed her phone flashing.

She picked it up and was upset to find four missed calls and three voicemail messages. *How the fuck did I miss them?* With increasing anxiety, she fumbled at the buttons until it unlocked, and the first voicemail was playing in her ear.

'This is a message from the Royal Hospital for Mrs. Sarah Todd. Can you please contact us immediately? There has been a development in your husband's case.'

'This is the Royal Hospital for Mrs. Sarah Todd. Please contact us immediately, on the following number, zero-one-two-one-one-two-two-three-seven-six-seven-eight. Ask for Doctor Powell.'

Cravings

'Mrs. Todd, please contact Doctor Powell immediately after receiving this message. Zero one two, double one double two three seven six seven eight. This is an urgent matter.'

Sarah's heart was beating faster than was healthy. *What could they want? He's only had a fall. A broken ankle or leg at the most!'*

In a blur, she dressed, grabbed the car keys, and drove to the hospital. Once there, she raced into a sparsely occupied reception.

A tired looking girl tried her best to smile at her. 'Can I help you?'

'Yes, I need to speak to Doctor Powell. He called me about my husband. He's had a fall.'

'One moment please,' she said as she regarded her computer screen. After a few moments, her face changed, becoming alert and business-like. 'Let me make a quick call. Can you take a seat for a moment?' The girl indicated a row of seats behind Sarah.

'No, I'm good, I just need to see Roger.'

The conversation on the phone lasted for less than a minute, then she turned back towards Sarah and smiled.

A professional smile if I've ever seen one, Sarah thought before finally sitting on the offered chairs.

A few minutes passed, then a man in a white coat made his way into the foyer. 'Mrs. Todd?' he asked, fixing the spectacles on his serious face.

'Yes, that's me. Can you tell me what this is about?'

'I'm sorry to have rang you so early in the morning. Can you follow me, please?'

'Doctor, I need to know what's happening. How is Roger?'

'Please, come into this office.' He led her into a small side room that consisted of a desk, two chairs, a telephone, and nothing else.

'I need to know how my husband is.'

Doctor Powell looked at her from the other side of the desk. His face was young, but she could see stresses on there that no one his age had any business having. 'I'm afraid I have some very bad news for you.'

Sarah's face fell as the words streamed from his mouth. Although she was expecting it after the frantic phone calls, hearing it was a different thing altogether.

'There was a complication. The break was worse than it seemed at the time. We believed that he was severely inebriated, due to the alcohol levels present in his blood. Although this *was* partly to blame, the real cause of his inability to communicate was due to the break of his tibia. Marrow fat from the bone was leaking directly into his blood stream, travelling directly to his brain. We believe a large fat cell caused a clot to form.'

Sarah regarded the doctor with wide eyes, the shock of what she was hearing all consuming. 'Is he…' she tried to say it but couldn't. The words just wouldn't form.

'Dead?' Doctor Powell continued. 'No, he's not dead. But he is in a vegetative state. He lost oxygen to the brain for too long. I'm so sorry, Mrs. Todd, but there is a slim chance of recovery.'

'Can I see him?' She was too shocked to cry. She suspected tears would come later, but now all she felt was numb.

'Of course, you can. It may be stressful for you to see him like this, his cranium has swollen. He is wearing a colostomy and a catheter; we just haven't had time to sort that yet.'

'I just need to see him, right now.'

The young doctor stood and indicated towards the door. 'Of course! If you'd follow me.'

They made their way through the hushed corridors until they came to a darkened room. There was a lot of electrical machinery and an odd hissing noise. Lying on a bed in the center of the room was a body, half covered in sheets, with lots of wires and cables attached to the machines around him.

'Remember, Mrs. Todd, this may be… traumatic.'

Sarah turned to face the doctor. 'Can I have some time alone?'

Powell adjusted his glasses. 'I'm not supposed to, but I'm sure I can make an exception on this occasion. Will an hour do you?'

She turned to look into the darkened room. 'Thank you, doctor.'

'Just don't touch anything in there; we're monitoring his vitals.'

'How long does he have?'

Powell shook his head. 'We don't know.'

She entered the room, closing the door behind her.

~~~~

The room was colder than she thought it would be. The man lying on the bed before her only resembled her husband and father to her unborn baby. His head was shaved, and there was bruising around his swollen features. But ultimately, she could tell it was him.

A tear pushed its way out of her eye and tracked down her face towards her lips. The moment she tasted the salty moisture, it opened the floodgates and was soon joined by many others.

Cravings

'Roger, you fucking idiot!' she sobbed. 'You know you can't drink! You selfish prick.' She was finding it difficult to breathe, the sobs were coming almost as fast as the tears. 'What am I going to do now? Eh? You're leaving me... with this...' She slapped her large belly, as if to emphasise it to him, in case he'd forgotten.

'Don't you dare fucking leave me! Don't you dare fucking...' she leaned forward, putting her face onto his chest. Grief had taken control, and before she knew it, she was hugging him. She looked towards door, relieved that no one had witnessed her small breakdown.

As she moved away from the bed, her arm connected with something; something that came away from whatever it was attached to.

Panicking, she checked to see what it was—she didn't want to be the cause of anything not working that might save his life. None of the machines were screaming, so she assumed that it hadn't been anything important.

Then the smell hit her.

The familiar sickly-sweet stink.

Something inside her stirred. Something that had been dormant for a while, something that she'd hoped had gone away.

Her stomach growled. It sounded angry.

Hunger descended upon her like a heavy blanket, blacking out all her senses, all her feelings, except for one.

The need to feed.

She sniffed for the source of the smell. Her investigations took her around to the other side of the bed, where she saw not only the source of the stench, but also what her arm had knocked.

It was the colostomy bag.

Pure, unprocessed waste was leaking from the white plastic bag, and from the tube that had been surgically inserted into his bowel.

Yellowing sludge dripped onto the bed, sinking into the sheets. She could smell it, raw and fresh, just how she liked it. The baby kicked as the abhorrent, but mouth-watering, fragrance hit her senses.

Acting on instinct, she began to lick the soiled sheets. The feel of the gunk on her tongue was exquisite, and she lapped at it like a thirsty dog at a puddle. The baby was turning somersaults inside her. She sucked on the cloth, extracting all of the delights from within the fibres.

Wiping the bed fluff from her mouth, she realised that something had awakened inside her, something that wouldn't go away until it was satisfied. She looked at the surgical bag. Sludge was still trickling from the tube. Without thinking, she took it and put it in her mouth and sucked on it, squeezing the bag like a child drinking a fruity drink from a straw.

Undiluted filth filled her mouth, and she revelled in it! As did her baby. She rinsed the slop around, savouring the concentrated flavour. As she swallowed, she clicked her tongue, relishing the tastes of the unoxygenated treat. Like a fine wine connoisseur, she strived to identify the different palates she was experiencing.

There was the hoppy taste of beer, not lager, but a real ale. There was also chicken curry in there too. They had obviously been to an Indian restaurant. As she sucked on her teeth, she guessed it had been something spicy, possibly a madras.

She squeezed the bag again, allowing more of the foul contents to squirt from the tube. Too much gushed out, and she almost choked as it went down the wrong pipe. She coughed, and a few droplets of grime fell from her nostrils. *I'll be smelling that for a week!* She laughed before continuing the disgusting meal.

The baby was loving it.

He, or she, was wriggling, as if dancing. 'Are you enjoying daddy?' she whispered, after swallowing another mouthful.

This thought made her sad, but what made her sadder was the fact that the small white bag was now empty, but the hunger inside her was far from satiated.

She needed more.

She thought about removing his catheter and drinking the dark yellow fluid that was inside, but she didn't think that would do her any good. Then she noticed the hole in her husband's stomach, where the colostomy bag had been pulled. It was leaking dark blood. Blood that was mixing with waste that had bypassed his bowels, destined for the bag.

In her twisted fever, she put her lips around the seeping hole and sucked. Blood filled her mouth, blood mixed with sweet, sweet shit. It was a whole new experience for her. The copper taste mixed with the nutty tinge of the faeces gave her baby a new lease of life. It spun and buckled inside her as she continued to feed.

Eventually, she had had her fill. Her clothes were covered in gore, as was her hair and face.

Without even thinking about her dying husband beneath her, she searched the room, looking for an exit. She needed something to hide her soiled clothing, but could find nothing that would cover the amount of filth she was coated in.

She poked her head out of the room and looked up and down the corridor; it was empty at this early hour. She crept out and headed towards the fire escape at the far end of the corridor. She pushed the door and was free, into the early morning air. It assaulted her nostrils, and her body attempted to reject the freshness as it craved more of the new-found elixir.

She found herself at the back of the hospital, not far from where the car was parked. She needed to get inside, and fast, before she was seen covered in her husband's filth.

Reaching the car, she relaxed with a long sigh of relief. But the smell of her breath set her stomach off again. The reek of effluence mixed with the copper tang of blood caused her baby to buck violently inside her.

It needed feeding again.

She gunned the engine and sped out of the hospital grounds.

7.

BY THE TIME she got home, there were four missed called from the hospital and three voicemail messages. All of them were from the same number as earlier.

She ignored them, removed her clothing, washed her face, and went straight to bed. She knew what they wanted anyway.

Roger was dead!

Boo-hoo!

She had a baby to feed.

~~~

Three men made from one-hundred-percent shit grabbed at her from bushes as she walked in the park. Instead of being scared, she welcomed them, relishing the feel of their slimy hands all over her body. She ripped open her own top, exposing her pregnant breasts, and leaking nipples, allowing the shit men to grope and cover her in their disgustingly beautiful paste.

She laid on the grass, enjoying the moist men tearing her clothes. She shivered as one of their heads snaked up between her thighs and licked the white cotton panties she was wearing. Her excitement heightened when a strong, yet soft, hand tore the now soiled, panties off her before a stinking, brown stained, tongue entered her.

Her orgasm was already rising.

The other two men were standing over her. They had removed their clothes and were both sporting thick, knotted turds as erections. One of them thrust his into her face, where she revelled in the putrid stink before grasping it and wrapping her lips around it. The log thickened in her mouth, and she flicked her tongue up and down the length, sucking on the slimy, brown head. Beautiful, stinking juice, like diarrhoea, ejaculated over her face in a beige shower, and she hungrily lapped it all into her waiting mouth. The second shit man was masturbating over her, and once she had finished with the first, she allowed him to cover her in his dysentery discharge.

It was in her hair. It was in her mouth. She could feel her baby twisting and turning, fancying that she heard it giggle. The love coming from it was warm and strong, just like the orgasm that was about to tear through her, from the shit man who was still performing cunnilingus with the wettest, softest tongue she had ever felt.

The orgasm shook her.

As she throbbed, she found herself turned over by the third shit man, and his turd like erection probed for her sphincter, which was now secreting, lubricating itself for the inevitable penetration.

When it came, it was unbelievable. She had never been fucked like this before, and she had time to wonder why before the third man ejaculated inside her. It was the reverse of passing a motion; it was like someone was passing it into her.

~~~~

She woke and was not at all surprised to find that she had defecated in the bed, and that she had half eaten the stool. The sheets were ruined, as were the bed clothes.

The clock on the side read four-thirty a.m.

She thought of the shit men and the taste of Roger's blood mixed with his faeces, and a plan hatched in her head.

She drove into town and parked.

It was five a.m. on a Sunday. There would not be many people about, which suited her needs completely.

Cravings

She checked the back seat of the car, making sure she had everything she needed.

She did!

8.

HER STOMACH GROWLED as she rested a hand on her bump and smiled. 'Not long now, baby, you're going to have everything you need, very soon.'

The public toilets in the centre of town were open twenty-four hours and manned by attendants much of the day, but she knew they wouldn't be manned now, not at this ungodly time in the morning.

She entered the conveniences and engaged the single baby changing cubicle at the end of the row.

She locked the door behind her and waited.

9.

AROUND SIX A.M., the sounds of someone entering the toilets roused her from a dreamless slumber. Whoever it was, they were shuffling about and mumbling to themselves. It was exactly what she needed.

A smell wafted through the room. It was dirty—sweat, filth, cheap wine, and greasy food. It was the stink of a homeless person.

Sarah could hear her hobbling around, looking in the bins and drinking from the water taps. She held her breath. Her stomach growled loudly, giving her game away.

'Who's there?' a toothless whisper hissed through the tiled room. 'I heard ya. Who's there?'

Sarah's heart thumped rapidly, her hands were clammy, and a sheen of sweat had drenched her.

'Come on! I won't hurt ya. Not if you give me a quid I won't…' The homeless person laughed.

Sarah poised herself. The kitchen knife she was holding felt slick in her sweaty hands. Her knuckles were white, almost translucent. *What the fuck am I doing here?* she thought. It was the first lucid thought she'd had in what seemed like such a long time. *I work in an accounts department. My husband has just died in hospital. I'm about to be a mother! Why am I in a public bathroom, holding a knife?*

Her stomach answered, letting loose another growl, a big one. She tasted bitter bile rising in her mouth. She was no longer hungry; she was ravenous!

She readjusted her grip on the knife.

'Jesus woman, that's some fart you did in there,' the homeless woman cackled. 'You're goin' be smelling worse than I do!'

Sarah kicked the cubicle door. There was a satisfying yelp as it banged into the woman hard, knocking her over. With a primal scream, she launched herself, landing on top of her victim, who shrieked in surprise.

The reek from this woman was repulsive, but then her stomach growled again, and it changed. It became delicious, like the smell of cooking bacon and maple syrup waffles.

'What the fuck?' the woman rasped in a toothless hiss.

Cravings

Sarah hit her with the hilt of the knife. The woman's grease bound hair hardly moved, but the bugs that were living within it did. Some of them flew, others scurried away like rats deserting a sinking ship.

She gripped the woman's dirty clothing and pulled her into the baby changing cubical. She offered little resistance. Sarah hit her again for good measure, then closed the door, locking them both inside.

'What do you want with me, lady? I've got no money.'

'I don't want money,' she snarled. 'I need you to shit for me.'

The homeless woman stopped whimpering and looked at the mad pregnant woman looming over her with the knife. 'You want me to what?'

'I want you to shit, you fucking tramp! Shit your pants, right now. Don't tell me you can't because I won't believe you.'

'I... I...' the woman stuttered.

Sarah hit her again. This time she allowed the blade to cut the woman's face a little, and the scratch began to bleed.

'Shit! Now!'

She sliced the woman's clothing, cutting from the top to the bottom, and the stinking rags fell away, revealing dishevelled, filthy, pale flesh beneath. Her skin was covered in rashes and scabs. Insect bites that looked infected covered her chest and breasts.

Sarah knelt next to the scared woman. The tramp was wearing a pair of large cotton pants that covered her stomach and both of her thighs. These were filthy too. Dark brown and yellow stains adorned the gusset, while others marked the back. Sarah's mouth moistened at the most depraved sight she had ever seen. She cut them, the knife making easy work of the worn fabric.

The poor woman shrank away, but Sarah grabbed her by the hair and steadied her.

The pants came away with ease.

In all the years of living on the streets in London, the woman had never, ever witnessed, or even heard of, what was happening to her right now.

Sarah picked up the soiled pants and brought them to her face, sniffing deeply at the gusset. She began to suck on them, stuffing them into her mouth, moaning with pleasure as the urine and menstrual stains that the homeless woman had been topping up for as long as she had been wearing them, possibly months, dissolved on her tongue. She began chewing at the back, picking off the dried flakes of shit with her teeth and chewing them as if they were a matured steak.

This was enough to make the homeless woman want to baulk.

This irony was not lost on her.

Once she had gotten what she needed from the pants, she turned her attention back onto the woman. She flashed the knife and leaned in close. 'Listen to me, you filthy little cunt. You're going to take a shit for me, right here, right now, on this floor. DO YOU HEAR ME?' she spat.

The woman nodded as she cowered.

'Good! Now get onto all fours, and really force one out. Do it now!' She sliced the woman's stomach, just a little, but enough to let her know that she wasn't joking.

The woman obeyed the strange order and turned onto all fours, weeping as she did. She flinched as she felt something probing at her back passage.

Sarah's heart was beating like a heavy metal band's drum at the sight of the woman on all fours. She lay the knife on the floor of the cubicle, keeping it within easy reach. She grabbed at the putrid, sore ridden, cheeks and dragged them apart, delighting in the stink that wafted from the scabby crack before she buried her face into the odorous crevice. The woman recoiled as Sarah's tongue reached out and licked the inside of her cheeks, lapping at her arse, which hadn't been cleaned, or even wiped properly, in a long time.

'Shit, goddam you!' Sarah ordered; her voice muffled by the woman's flesh. 'Shit now or I'll fucking cut you!'

She felt the woman strain.

A small bout of gas seeped through the tight muscle, and she opened her mouth hoping to catch whatever was coming next. But nothing else escaped the filthy starfish. 'Push again… NOW!' she snarled.

The woman strained again, and more gas erupted, this time accompanied by a trickle of anal juice. It was thick and green, almost like phlegm. Sarah caught it in her mouth as it seeped from the source and swallowed it, much to the delight of the baby in her stomach. 'More… I need more.'

The petrified homeless woman strained one last time.

Sarah marvelled at the opening of the hole before her, and the emergence of a stool popping its small brown head through. It looked like something from one of the rubbish science fiction movies Roger used to make her watch.

Congratulations, it's a shit, she laughed in her head as the woman pushed again. Eventually, the rest of the stool struggled through, followed by a wet release of air and a stream of foul smelling but delicious sap, exploding over her welcoming face.

Cravings

The woman was crying now, but Sarah didn't care. She was too busy pushing her face into, and enjoying, the warm excrement.

Another wet explosion from the foul backside spewed forth another feast for her delectation.

She picked up the slippery turd from the floor and regarded it. It was fantastic, her baby thought so too, as it began to spin in her stomach, delighting Sarah in its healthy acrobatics.

She took a bite out of it. It was tougher than she thought it would be coming from such a disgusting individual, and she savoured it. Who knew that greasy fast food and alcohol made for fantastic, flavoured shit?

'Turn over!' she demanded of the woman.

When the woman looked at the mad lady with the shit over her face, her world collapsed, and her already thin hold on reality flipped. 'Whoa! Listen, you're into some weird shit, and I mean that literally. Now… please, let me get dressed, and we can forget all about this, eh? Can we?'

Sarah stared at the woman while brown filth dripped from her face and hands. She reached for the knife. 'Something is missing!' she whispered. 'There's something else that I need, something else my baby needs! Something we had last night.'

She plunged the knife into the homeless woman's stomach, and a stream of blood gushed from her, as did a guttural scream.

Sarah panicked, thinking someone might have heard and would come to help, disturbing her feast, so she took the knife and slit the woman's throat. The blade was sharp, and the cut didn't take much effort at all.

The woman's struggles died with her, leaving Sarah to enjoy her meal with no interruptions. She mixed the blood and shit lying pooled around her until it turned black, then licked it up from the floor. Guttural animal noises emanated from her as she and the baby relished every last speck of their meal.

When the floor was clean, she still needed more. She picked up the knife and made an educated guess as the where the woman's bowel would be, where the lion's share of this woman's undigested materials would be stored.

She hit the jackpot first time.

Fresh blood slewed onto the floor, followed by gore and innards.

Sarah buried her head into the woman's stomach, searching for more.

~~~

So engrossed in her meal was she, that she didn't hear the cleaner enter to start her day.

Cravings

She didn't hear the woman shout, scream, and then run out of the toilets.

She also didn't hear the woman return with police escorts. Their radio calls for backup also failed to fall upon her blood and shit filled ears.

In fact, the only time she noticed anyone else was in the room with her was when, finally satisfied, she sat back, leaning against the gore spattered wall, and saw the armed police pointing their guns at her.

A soiled smile crept over her face as she pointed to her belly.

'I've got cravings,' she mumbled.

10.

TWO WEEKS LATER, Sarah was in the hospital, screaming for medication and rattling handcuffs on the metal frame of the bed she was in.

It was a rudimentary birthing bed in the hospital wing of a high security mental health facility.

Forty-five minutes of agony later, she gave birth to a healthy baby.

~~~~

Screaming was coming from somewhere not too far away. *That can't be my baby,* she thought.

Her head was fuzzy these days.

No, it can't be my baby! Roger would be here if it was, along with my mother and sister. Wouldn't they?

Cravings

A nurse, dressed in green scrubs and a white mask and carrying a bundle of white materials, stained pink in places, leaned into her.

'It's a girl,' she whispered. 'Would you like to see her?'

Sarah nodded, wondering why this stranger was about to show her someone else's baby, but she wanted to see anyway.

As the nurse opened the bundle, a small, naked, pink child, complete with umbilical cord still attached, gargled.

Sarah smiled as a tear trickled down her cheek.

Just as the baby was being wrapped back up, its little face went bright red, and it looked like it was forcing something out.

A black, sticky substance slid down the baby's leg.

Sarah's eyes went wide, and her mouth filled with saliva…

D E McCluskey

Cravings

Authors Notes

WELL, THIS STORY is a tough read, even for me, and I wrote it!

I know there is a huge, and I do mean massive, market for extreme horror, splatter punk, body shock, and the likes. However, I can hold my hand in the air and say that I've never, really, been a fan of these more extreme sides of horror. I've read the likes of Matt Shaw, David Charlesworth, and a few of the others, and I have enjoyed their work, it is a definite and legitimate art form, and some people can get it so right, but it's mostly not my cup of tea.

I toyed with the idea of writing extreme horror when I produced my novel CRACK, but in the end, I toned it down and removed some of the more extreme gore. I felt the story was the better for it, as I think the extreme parts of it were detrimental to the story, kind of overpowering the story I was trying to portray.

So, this tale is probably the closest I've gotten to writing extreme horror, even though I think it has ended up more scatological than extreme.

Anyhoos… I have no control over what the muse wants me to write, so if the story is in there, then it must come out, one way or the other.

I originally wrote this for an anthology I was going to work on with Matt Shaw, however, it never really panned out (we were going to call it Shit Stories to read on the Toilet). So, it's kind of languished, floated if you would, around for a while, not doing anything.

However, I really liked it, in a weird kind of way, and wanted it to get some distribution… so I have produced it as a novelette (I have never even heard of a novelette until about two weeks ago), and bunged it up on Amazon for a laugh…

I hope you enjoy it, more than I do anyway!

Thanks go out to Tony Higginson, for shaping it into a real short story. Lisa Lee Tone for editing it so it kind of makes sense… Lauren Davies just for the support. Normally, she would have been

Cravings

a proof-reader (the final one), but she chickened out when I told her what the subject matter was.

Lastly, but not leastly… is YOU, the readers. I don't care how sick and twisted you are, I love you all for taking the time and reading this short work of vileness.

Keep it up, otherwise I will end up going mad with all these tales banging around in my head.

Dave McCluskey
Liverpool
May 2021

Printed in Great Britain
by Amazon